THE FIRST
FANGS-GIVING

THE FIRST FANGS-GIVING

BY MICHELLE POPLOFF

ILLUSTRATED BY BILL BASSO

SCHOLASTIC INC.

New York   Toronto   London   Auckland   Sydney

Mexico City   New Delhi   Hong Kong   Buenos Aires

With all my love to Daniel and Leanne.
Every day I give thanks for you.

—M. P.

To my pal Sal

—B. B.

ISBN-13: 978-0-439-28913-9
ISBN-10: 0-439-28913-0

Text copyright © 2001 by Michelle Poploff.
Illustrations copyright © 2001 by Bill Basso.
All rights reserved. Published by Scholastic Inc.
SCHOLASTIC and associated logos are trademarks
and/or registered trademarks of Scholastic Inc.

12 11 10 9 8 7 6   7 8 9 10 11 12/0

Printed in the U.S.A.   40
First Scholastic printing, November 2001

CONTENTS

Chapter 1
WANDA'S WIGGLY, JIGGLY TOOTH

Wanda Doomsday was trying hard to
listen to Mrs. Bono talk about
Thanksgiving.
But she couldn't help wiggling and
jiggling in her seat.
Wanda was so excited about her loose
tooth.
It was right next to her front fang.

Wanda jiggled the tooth with her finger.
She quietly sneaked a piece of popcorn
from her snack bag.

Maybe if she chewed a piece, her tooth
would fall out right now.

No one had ever lost a tooth in class
before.

"Wanda Doomsday," said Mrs. Bono,
"can you answer the question?"

Uh-oh, thought Wanda.

She hid the popcorn in her fist.

She cleared her throat.

"Well, um," she said, wishing she could
remember the question.

"We're waiting, Wanda," said Mrs. Bono.
"Can you name something that Squanto
and his Native American friends helped
the Pilgrims to plant?"

"Popcorn," Wanda blurted out. "They planted popcorn."

The class burst out laughing.

"Planting popcorn!" said Wayne the
Pain Dobbs. "That's a new one, Wanda.
I'll have to remember that."
Wanda slid down in her seat.
"I meant to say that they planted *corn*,"
she said in a small voice.
Wanda thought a moment.
"When the corn grew, they picked it,"
she went on. "Then they could make
popcorn from that."

Mrs. Bono smiled.

"Corn is correct," she said. "It was very valuable to the Native Americans and the Pilgrims. We'll add it to our list."

Sheesh, thought Wanda. *How come I always get called on when I don't raise my hand?*

She opened her fist.

Her palm was sweaty and the popcorn was crumbled.

"How else did the Native Americans help the Pilgrims?" Mrs. Bono asked.

Wanda's good friend, Helen Hooper, raised her hand.

"The Native Americans taught the Pilgrims to hunt and fish," she said.

"Very good," said Mrs. Bono, writing on the board.

Wanda thought of something else.

She raised her hand.

So did Wayne.

Mrs. Bono called on Wayne.

"The Native Americans showed the Pilgrims where to find nuts and berries in the forest," he said.

"That's right, Wayne," said Mrs. Bono. "Did you have something else to add, Wanda?"

Wanda scowled at Wayne.

That was exactly what she was going to

say.

"Not anymore," said Wanda.

She looked at her witch watch.

It was almost noon.

Maybe her loose tooth would fall out

during lunch.

Chapter 2
PARTY PLANNERS

After lunch, Mrs. Bono had a surprise for the class.

"Since Thanksgiving is just a few days away," she said, "I think it would be fun for our class to have our own first Thanksgiving feast."

"Hooray!" the kids shouted.

Just then, Principal Shaw walked into the room.

He asked Mrs. Bono to step outside for a moment.

"Excuse me, class," their teacher said. "Helen, would you please lead our discussion until I return?"

Helen nodded.

"We could talk about what we're thankful for at our feast," she said.

"I have a better idea," said Buffy. "We could dress up as Pilgrims and Native Americans. I'll come as the Pilgrim parent in charge of all the Pilgrim children. I can wear my fancy, red velvet cape," she said, smiling at the class.

What nerve, thought Wanda. *That Buffy is so bossy.*

"My cape is ten times better," said Wanda. "It even has secret pockets."

She patted her black cape and swished it around herself.

Buffy shook her head at Wanda.

"You call that a Pilgrim cape?" she squeaked.

"It's more Pilgrim-ish than yours any day," said Wanda.

"Forget about being a Pilgrim, Wanda," said Hector. "Remember when we learned about Pocahantas? You could come as Poca-*haunt*-us."

Hector cracked up at his own joke.

"Well," said Wanda, "you won't need a costume, Hector, since you're already the class turkey!"

"That's a gobble-gobble good one," said Wayne.

Everyone was laughing when Mrs. Bono returned.

"What were you talking about?" she asked.

"Turkey," said Helen. "Wanda just mentioned turkey."

"Perfect," said Mrs. Bono. "We need to discuss what everyone can bring. Who thinks their parents or grandparents can help out?"

Several children, including Wanda, raised their hands.

Wanda reached over and tapped Helen on the head with her pencil.

"I'm going to eat lots of corn on the cob at our Thanksgiving feast," Wanda said, as she jiggled her tooth. "That should do the trick."

"Why does your tooth have to fall out for Thanksgiving?" Helen asked.
"Simple," said Wanda. "Then I'll have something to be *fang*-ful for."

MAYFLOWER

Chapter 3
SOMETHING FISHY GOING ON

Over the next few days, Mrs. Bono's
class wrote about the Pilgrims and
Native Americans working together.
They decorated the room with drawings
of them hunting and fishing, planting
and feasting.

"I'm sure your relatives will want to hear
some interesting facts about the first
Thanksgiving," said Mrs. Bono.

A tiny bell went off in Wanda's head
upon hearing her teacher's words.
Yes! she thought. *I need an interesting fact
that we haven't read about in class. But what?*

After school, Wanda went home and
began reading.
Curled up on her bed, she tried to picture
herself as a Pilgrim living long ago.
Soon she learned something very
interesting that she didn't know before.

The next morning, Wanda put something extra in her backpack. While the other kids read their poems and stories, Wanda waited for her turn. She was so excited, she forgot about wiggling her loose tooth.

When Buffy finished reading her poem, she headed back to her desk.

As she passed Wanda, she stopped and sniffed.

"*Pee-uuw*, Wanda!" cried Buffy. "What's that smell?"

All the kids looked at Wanda.

"It's for my Pilgrim project," she said, reaching into her backpack. "I brought a fish."

Wanda held up a plastic bag with a flounder in it.

By now, all the kids around her were holding their noses.

"I think you should go next, Wanda," said Mrs. Bono.

"So do I," said Wanda, walking to the front of the room with the fish.

"I read that the Native Americans put fish in the ground when they planted their seeds," Wanda began proudly. "The fish made the soil better for growing corn."

"But it stinks," said Wayne. He held a handkerchief to his nose. "Can stinky fish make corn grow, Mrs. Bono?"

"What do you think, Wanda?" asked Mrs. Bono, opening the classroom door.

"I think it definitely helped the soil," Wanda answered with confidence. "The Native Americans and Pilgrims had plenty of corn and other food for their Thanksgiving feast."

"That's good work, Wanda," said Mrs. Bono. "Now let's find a place to put that fish."

Wanda grinned and wiggled her loose tooth.

Chapter 4
THE NATIVE AMERICAN PRINCESS

Wanda jumped out of bed on the day
of the class Thanksgiving feast.
She quickly got dressed, saving the
best for last.
She didn't care about Buffy being a
Pilgrim in her fancy, red cape.
Wanda was going as a Native American
Princess.
The night before, she had made a
headdress by gluing brightly colored
feathers onto a headband.

When she put it on, Wanda knew this was a better choice than wearing a plain, white Pilgrim's cap.

GREEN CREAM

"Wahoo, Wanda," said her brother, Artie, at breakfast. "You are one weird-looking Native American."

"*Fangs* very much, Artie," she said, reaching for some ghost toast with booberry jelly.

"Speaking of fangs," said Artie, "what has webbed feet and fangs?"

"Whump?" asked Wanda while chewing.

"Count Quackula," he said.

"I almost forgot," yelled Wanda, dropping her ghost toast. "*Fangs* for reminding me."

She ran to her room and stuffed a bag into her backpack.

"I hope that's not more dead fish," said Artie. "You stunk up the whole school."

Wanda giggled.

"I was just giving a history lesson. See you at school, Granny," she called out.
"I'll be there, dearie," Granny called back.
"Save me some corn bread," said Artie.

Chapter 5
WE GATHER TOGETHER

All the children in Mrs. Bono's class were busy moving chairs and desks and setting up plates and cups.

Wanda the Native American Princess and Buffy the Pilgrim parent came face-to-face.

Mrs. Bono placed a hand on each girl's shoulder.

"If the Pilgrims and Native Americans could be friends, why don't you two give it a try," she said.

The girls nodded.

"Funky feathers," Buffy said to Wanda.

"Cute cap," Wanda said to Buffy.

"Good," said Mrs. Bono. "Here are some parents and grandparents now."

The children formed lines while the grown-ups served the delicious food. While they were eating, Granny Doomsday said, "How about a quick holiday riddle-go-round?"

"Good idea!" said Mrs. Bono. "Who
will get us started?"
Wanda jumped up.
"I will!" she shouted. "Knock, knock."
"Who's there?" said Buffy.
"Wanda."
Buffy looked puzzled.
"Wanda who?" she asked.
"Wanda try some pumpkin pie?" said
Wanda, giggling.

Buffy laughed.

"It's yummy," she said, "but my mom was really mad when she made it."

"Why do you say that?" asked Wanda.

"Because she beat the eggs and whipped the cream," Buffy answered with a grin.

Wanda laughed so hard she had to take a long drink of Hector's spicy apple spider. Even Mrs. Bono joined in the fun.

"What animal can jump higher than this school?" she asked.

No one knew the answer.

"Any animal," said Mrs. Bono. "This school can't jump."

"Good one, Mrs. Bono," the kids called out.

"Thank you," their teacher said. "Now who wants to pull the wishbone?"

Wanda and Buffy raised their hands
first.

Mrs. Bono asked them both to step
forward.

Hooray for me! Wanda thought. *I finally
got called on when I raised my hand.*

"Now each of you make a wish and
pull your piece when I say go," said
Mrs. Bono.

Wanda wished her wiggly tooth would
fall out right then and there.

The girls pulled at the wishbone.

Buffy got the larger piece.

Wanda stamped her foot.

Buffy backed away.

No fair, thought Wanda, as she plopped into her seat.

She was chewing her last bite of turkey when she felt something hard in her mouth.

Maybe it was a tiny turkey bone.

She spit it into her hand.

"Look, everyone!" Wanda shouted. "There's a tooth in my turkey!"

"Gross, Wanda," said Buffy. "There's blood on it."

Wanda looked closely at her tooth.

"That's not blood," she said. "It's cranberry sauce."

She wrapped her tooth in a napkin and put it in her pocket.

It will go under her pillow tonight.

Chapter 6
A HAPPY FANGS-GIVING

Everyone pitched in and helped
clean up.

Soon the room looked like a classroom
again.

"Now that we've eaten that tasty meal,"
said Mrs. Bono, "the children will talk
about our country's first Thanksgiving
and what we have to be thankful for."

Wanda raised her hand.

"May I please go first?" she asked.

It felt funny talking with her tooth
missing.

Hector held his nose.

"Get ready for the dead fish," he said.

"Not this time," said Wanda.

She opened the bag she packed that morning.

"Everyone knows Thanksgiving is a time for giving thanks. Since I'm Wanda Doomsday, I'm giving *fangs* for all my friends. Even you, Hector."

"That's my girl," cheered Granny. Wanda passed the fake fangs to all the kids and even the grown-ups.

HAPPY FANGS-GIVING FROM THE DOOMSDAYS!